D0464909

Palo Alto City Library

The individual borrower is responsible for all library material borrowed on his or her card.

Charges as determined by the CITY OF PALO ALTO will be assessed for each overdue item.

Damaged or non-returned property will be billed to the individual borrower by the CITY OF PALO ALTO.

P.O. Box 10250, Palo Alto, CA 94303

THE WEEPING
WILLOW

OTHER IKE AND MEM STORIES

The Bird Shadow

The Tornado Watches

THE WEEPING WILLOW

An Ike and Mem Story

BY Patrick Jennings

ILLUSTRATED BY
Anna Alter

HOLIDAY HOUSE / NEW YORK

Library of Congress Cataloging-in-Publication Data
Jennings, Patrick.
The weeping willow / by Patrick Jennings;
illustrated by Anna Alter.— 1st ed.
p. cm. — (An Ike and Mem story; 3)
Summary: While trying to build a tree house for guys,
Ike and his best friend, Buzzy, argue so much that Ike builds his sister
Mem a playhouse instead, but still misses his friend.
ISBN 0-8234-1671-2
[1. Interpersonal relations—Fiction. 2. Brothers and sisters—Fiction.
3. Best friends—Fiction. 4. Friendship—Fiction.
5. Tree houses—Fiction.] I. Alter, Anna, ill.
II. Title.

PZ7.J4298715 We 2002
[E]—dc21

2002020544

For Odette
and the park across the street
—P. J.

For Amiko
—A. A.

Ike and Mem and Ike's best friend, Buzzy Starzinsky, were fishing in the pond.

"I still think deviled ham works best," Buzzy said.

"I've caught more fish," Ike said.

"But they were all too small to keep," Buzzy said. "Only little fish like bologna."

Ike lifted his line. A tiny bluegill flipped and flopped at the end of it.

"See?" Buzzy said.

Ike reeled in his line, unhooked the fish, and threw it back in the water.

"Help!" called Mem suddenly. "Help, help!"

"Mem?" Ike called back, dropping his pole. "Where are you, Mem?"

"I'm right here!"

"Right where?"

"Right *here!*"

"There she is!" Buzzy said, pointing. "Over in the cattails!"

Ike ran to where she was, stepped into the water, and pulled her out. His pants got muddy up to the knees. His shoes got soaked. Mem was muddy up to her elbows.

"What were you doing?" Ike asked.

"I wanted a corn dog," Mem said.

"Those aren't corn dogs," Buzzy said. "Those are cattails."

Mem looked at the cattails. "Where are the rest of the cats?"

Buzzy laughed.

"They're not real cats' tails," Ike said. "They just look like them."

"Oh," Mem said. "Can I have one?"

"You shouldn't be going in the water," Buzzy said. "There's a snapping turtle in there. It could bite off your leg."

"Don't tell her that," Ike said. "It's not true, Mem."

"Yes, it is," Buzzy said.

"No, it isn't," Ike said.

"Yes, it is," Buzzy said.

"Can you get a cattail for me, Ike?" Mem asked.

"Yeah, go ahead, Ike," Buzzy said with a grin.

"Since there isn't a snapping turtle in there."

"Okay," Ike said.

He stepped into the water. When he reached up for a cattail, he lost his balance and slipped all the way under the water. When he came back up, he was covered with mud.

Buzzy laughed and laughed.

"Let's go home," Ike grumbled.

"Did you get my corn dog?" Mem asked.

Buzzy laughed so hard that he fell down.

They walked home across the open field behind the hospital. The sun was hot. It dried Ike's mud.

"You look like a salamander," Mem said to him.

Buzzy laughed. He was having a fun day.

They passed the old weeping willow tree in the middle of the field. Its branches drooped to the ground all the way around.

"Can we go inside the weeping willow tree?" Mem asked.

"No," Ike said. The mud on his cheeks cracked. "I want to go home."

"Come on," Buzzy said. "It's hot out. It'll be cool in there."

"Oh, all right," Ike said. The mud on his neck cracked. "But just for a minute."

They parted the drooping branches and stepped in. It was much cooler under the tree. Mem ran around and around inside the curtain of drooping branches, singing:

"Ring inside the willow, a pocketful of pillows. Ashes, ashes, we all fall *down!*"

Then she fell onto her back on the ground.

"This would be a great place for a tree house," Buzzy said to Ike. "No one would ever know about it. We could use pieces from our old one."

Ike and Buzzy had once had a tree house in Ike's backyard. Then one day a tornado knocked down the tree it was in. The tree house was smashed to pieces.

"I'll help!" Mem chirped from the ground.

Buzzy frowned. "No, Mem," he said. "It's going to be a *guy* tree house. Right, Ike?"

Mem looked up at Ike.

"I guess so," he said. The mud on his forehead cracked.

"So I can't go in it?" Mem said.

"I'll build you a playhouse in the backyard," Ike said.

Mem's chin quivered. She was going to cry.

"You can invite your friends over to play in it," Ike said. "You can have a tea party."

A tear ran down Mem's cheek.

"I hate tea," she said.

The sky turned gray as they were walking home across the open field. Then it began to rain. Ike, Mem, and Buzzy ran fast through the tall grass. Thunder rumbled overhead.

"We're going to get hit by lightning!" Buzzy yelled.

"We're okay!" Ike yelled back. "We're wearing tennis shoes!"

"That doesn't matter!" Buzzy yelled.

"Yes, it does!" Ike yelled.

"No, it doesn't!" Buzzy yelled.

"I'm not wearing tennis shoes!" Mem yelled. She was wearing her tap shoes.

Ike stopped running. He handed Buzzy his fishing pole and tackle box. Then he picked up Mem and put her on his back.

"Giddyap!" Mem said.

Ike galloped toward home.

When they got there, Ike's mother told them they had to take baths. Mem went first. Ike heard her talking to herself in the tub.

"This is a *girl* bath," she said. "No guys, and no tea."

The next day Ike and Buzzy started bringing their stuff out to the weeping willow tree. They brought out broken plywood sheets and splintered two-by-fours. They brought out the old crate they'd used for a table in their tree house. They brought out the big wooden spools that they'd used for stools. They brought out their tool chests. They brought out their school lunch boxes. They did not bring out Mem.

"I think that branch is the best for the tree house," Buzzy said.

"It's not strong enough," Ike said.

"Yes, it is," Buzzy said.

"No, it isn't," Ike said.

"Yes, it is," Buzzy said.

"No, it isn't," Ike said.

"I'm hungry," Buzzy said. "I'm ready for our lunch break."

"Me too," Ike said.

They sat on the ground and opened their lunch boxes. Ike had a bologna sandwich. Buzzy had deviled ham. He also had potato chips. Ike had forgotten his.

"I'd give you some," Buzzy said, "except I'm starving."

"I'd give you some if I had some and you didn't," Ike said.

"No, you wouldn't," Buzzy said.

"Yes, I would," Ike said.

"No, you wouldn't," Buzzy said.

"Oh, forget it," Ike said.

Ike had milk in his thermos. Buzzy had forgotten to fill his. Ike said he would give Buzzy some except he was dying of thirst. They argued some more, then they stopped talking to each other.

They sawed two-by-fours into short pieces without talking. They nailed the boards to the tree trunk without talking. They carried the floor up and nailed it to the tree in silence. Then they silently put up the supports and the walls. Finally, Buzzy spoke.

"That wall is crooked," he said.

"No, it isn't," Ike said.

"Yes, it is."

"No, it isn't."

"Oh, never mind," Buzzy said.

While they were carrying the roof up the steps, the wind began to blow. The tree shook. The drooping branches waved and swooshed. Ike felt a drop of water on his nose.

"It's raining," he said.

"No, it isn't," Buzzy said.

Ike felt a drop on his head. But he didn't say anything. He was sick of arguing.

The wind blew harder. Ike and Buzzy couldn't hold onto the roof. It blew out of their hands and crashed into pieces on the ground.

"I'm ready to quit for the day," Ike said.

"Fine by me," Buzzy said.

They put away their tools. They picked up their tool chests and their lunch boxes. Then they parted the drooping branches and stepped outside. It wasn't raining.

They walked home ten feet apart. They didn't talk.

Mem was in the backyard when Ike got home. She had her play tools out: her plastic hammer, plastic screwdriver, and plastic saw. She was hammering on a scrap of wood that Ike and Buzzy had left behind.

"What are you doing?" Ike yelled over the hammering.

"I can't hear you!" Mem yelled back. "I'm hammering!"

"Can you stop for a minute?" Ike yelled.

"What?" Mem yelled. She stopped hammering. "I couldn't hear you. I was hammering."

"What are you building?" Ike asked.

"A girl tree house," Mem said.

"Oh," Ike said. "Do you want some help?"

"You're a guy," Mem said. "You can't help."

"Oh," Ike said again. "You don't have any nails, you know."

"Do I need nails?"

"Yes," Ike said. "You need nails. I have some. And I have my real tools. Do you want me to help?"

"You're a guy," Mem said again.

"Yeah, but I'm a *brother* guy. It's okay if I'm a brother guy."

"But I'm a *sister* girl," Mem said, "and I can't help you."

"That's because you're a *little*-sister girl,"

Ike explained. "I'm an *older*-brother guy, which is different."

Mem squinted at him. "Are you sure?" she asked.

"Positive," Ike said.

"Okay," Mem said. "Give me some nails."

"I'll do the nails," Ike said. "You'll hurt yourself."

"It's my tree house," Mem said. "I'll do the nails." And she held out her hand.

Ike sighed, then gave her a nail. She set it on the board and swatted at it with her plastic hammer.

"Ooh!" she squealed. "I hit my knuckle!"

Ike didn't say "I told you so."

"You do the nails," Mem said, sucking her knuckle.

Ike got out his tools and started building.

"I'm going to build you a playhouse," he said as he worked. "One that sits on the ground. You're not big enough for a tree house."

"We don't have a tree anyway," Mem said. "It fell down."

"Right," Ike said.

"Where's Buzzy?" Mem asked. "Why aren't you guys playing together?"

"We don't play together," Ike said. "We hang out."

"Oh," Mem said. "Why aren't you guys hanging out?"

"I got sick of hanging out with him."

"Did he get sick of hanging out with you too?" Mem asked.

Ike shrugged. "I guess so," he said.

"You ready?" Buzzy asked Ike the next morning. He was standing on the other side of Ike's screen door.

"I'm ready," Ike said.

They walked across the open field behind the hospital to the weeping willow tree. It was hot out. They didn't talk.

They got to work fixing the roof. When they were finished, they carried it up the steps. The wind started to blow again. The tree shook. The drooping branches waved and swooshed. Ike felt a drop on his hand.

"It's raining," he said.

"No, it isn't," Buzzy said.

Ike felt a drop on his shoulder.

"Yes, it is," he said.

"No, it isn't," Buzzy said.

Ike felt one on his lip. He licked it. It tasted salty, like sweat, or a tear.

The wind blew harder. Ike and Buzzy could not hold onto the roof and it crashed into pieces on the ground.

"I'm hungry," Buzzy said.

"We just started," Ike said.

"It's too windy to work," Buzzy said. "I'm taking my lunch break."

They sat on the floor of the tree house and ate their lunches. They both had potato chips and milk this time. They ate without talking.

Then Ike saw a drop splash on his lunch box.

"It's raining," he said.

Buzzy just rolled his eyes. "It's sunny out," he said. "Look."

Ike got up and stepped through the branches. There wasn't a cloud in the sky. He went back inside and sat down on the roof. He touched the drop on his lunch box with his finger. Then he touched the drop to his tongue. It tasted salty, like sweat, or a tear. He remembered the tear that had run down Mem's face.

"Maybe the tree is crying," Ike said.

Buzzy rolled his eyes again.

"Maybe we're hurting it," Ike said to himself.

The wind died down after lunch. Ike and Buzzy fixed the roof again, then they carried it up into the tree. They set it on top of the tree house.

"Finally!" Buzzy said with a sigh.

Then the wind started blowing again. The tree shook. The drooping branches waved and swooshed. Ike felt a drop on his cheek. He stuck out his tongue and licked it. It tasted salty.

"The tree is crying again," he said.

"It is not!" Buzzy said.

"It is!" Ike said back.

"Oh, I quit!" Buzzy yelled.

He climbed down the tree and started gathering up his tools.

"That's *my* screwdriver!" Ike said.

"No, it isn't!"

"Yes, it is!"

Buzzy looked at it. "Big deal!" he said, and threw it on the ground. Then he parted the drooping branches and stepped outside. They swung shut behind him.

Ike climbed down and got his hammer. Then he climbed back up and started knocking down the tree house. He knocked down the roof and the walls and the floor. Then he pulled out the steps with the hammer's claw. He put his tools away and picked up his tool chest and his lunch box. He parted the drooping branches and stepped outside. They swung shut behind him.

"Older-brother guy!" Mem called to him from the backyard. "Older-brother guy! I need your help!"

She was hammering with her plastic hammer.

"You need nails," Ike said.

"It hurts when I use nails," Mem said.

Ike got back to work on the playhouse. He had already made the floor, so he started on the walls.

At noon his mother called them in for lunch. Ike kept working. He had already eaten. Soon he ran out of wood, so he walked across the open field behind the hospital to the weeping willow tree. He gathered up as much wood as he could and carried it home. When he needed more, he went back across the field. Hours later there was no wood left under the weeping willow tree and the playhouse was built.

"Let's paint it!" Mem said.

"Okay," Ike said. "What color?"

"*All* colors!" Mem said.

They got paint out of the garage. There were cans of white paint, green paint, and yellow paint.

"Is that enough colors?" Ike said.

"No," Mem said, "but we'll have to make do."

They painted the house white, green, and

yellow. They painted one of the spools white, the other green, and the table yellow.

When the paint was dry, Mem went into the house and got her tea service. She sat down on the green spool.

"Care for some tea?" she asked Ike.

"I thought you hated tea," Ike said.

"This is pretend tea," Mem said. "One lump or two?"

"Three," Ike said, and sat down on the white spool.

"You ready?" Buzzy asked the next morning. He was standing on the other side of Ike's screen door.

"Ready for what?" Ike asked.

"Ready to work on our tree house," Buzzy said.

"I don't want to," Ike said. "It makes the tree cry. It makes Mem cry too."

"Mem always cries," Buzzy said.

"No, she doesn't," Ike said with a scowl.

They didn't talk for a minute, then Buzzy said, "You're really not coming?"

"I'm not coming," Ike said.

"Then I'm going to build it myself!" Buzzy said. He turned and walked away.

"There's no more stuff out there!" Ike called after him. "I carried it all home!"

Buzzy stopped. He turned back around. "You carried it home?"

Ike nodded.

"You carried it home without talking to *me*?" Buzzy asked.

Ike nodded again. "I built Mem a playhouse with it."

Buzzy's mouth fell open.

"Do you want to see it?" Ike asked. "It's out back."

"You built Mem a playhouse with *our* stuff?" Buzzy asked.

Ike sighed. "Yes," he said. "It's all painted and everything. Come and see it."

"Forget you!" Buzzy said, and he stomped away.

Ike went out the back door. Mem was in the playhouse.

"Where's Buzzy?" she asked. "Aren't you guys hanging out?"

"No," Ike said.

"Are you still sick of it?"

"Yes."

"Do you want some tea?"

"No."

"I don't either. I don't like tea. Even pretend tea. How about some coffee? It's decaf."

Ike smiled. "Okay," he said.

He played with Mem in the playhouse all

morning. They had coffee. They had cocoa. They had pizza. They had dandelion soup. Then they went into the real house for real lunch. They had bologna sandwiches, potato chips, and milk. Mem picked out the bologna from her sandwich.

After lunch Ike got his fishing pole and tackle box and walked next door. He knocked on the screen door. Buzzy's mother answered.

"Hi, Ike," she said. "I'll get him."

"Thanks, Mrs. Starzinsky," Ike said.

She went away, then Buzzy came to the door.

"What?" he said through the screen.

"Want to go fishing?" Ike asked.

"Why don't you ask Mem?" Buzzy said. "You can catch her some *corn dogs*."

"So you don't want to?" Ike asked.

"No," Buzzy said.

Ike looked down at his shoes. "I'm sorry about not talking to you about our stuff," he said. Then he turned and ran away down the sidewalk.

Ike didn't go fishing. He didn't feel like it anymore. He didn't feel like reading or watching baseball on TV either. He didn't feel like anything. He lay down on his bed and stared at the ceiling.

Then Mem came into his room.

"What are you doing?" she asked.

"Nothing," Ike said.

"Is Buzzy sick?"

"No."

"Did he have to go somewhere?"

"No."

"Are you sick?"

"No."

"Are you sick of hanging out with him?"

"I guess so," Ike said.

"Want some decaf?" Mem asked.

Ike laughed. "Sure."

Ike and Mem pretended to drink coffee in her playhouse. Then Mem pretended to make a coffee cake. Ike pretended to eat it.

"How is it?" Mem asked.

"Good," Ike said, pretending his mouth was full.

Mem smiled.

"Anybody home?" a voice called from outside. It was Buzzy's voice.

Mem stuck her head out the window. "It's Buzzy," she said.

Ike stuck his head out the other window.

"Nice playhouse," Buzzy said.

"Ike made it," Mem said. "I helped, though. I painted."

"Can I come in?" Buzzy asked.

"It's a *girl* playhouse," Mem said.

"What about Ike?"

"He's an older-brother guy," Mem said. "Which is different."

"*I'm* an older guy," Buzzy said.

"But you're not an older-*brother* guy," Mem said.

"Best friends of older-brother guys are okay, Mem," Ike said.

"Are you sure?" Mem asked, squinting.

"Positive," Ike said.

"See?" Buzzy said. "Deviled ham works better!"

A big bluegill flipped and flopped at the end of his line. He reeled in the fish, then unhooked it.

"It's huge!" he said.

Right then the bluegill flopped very hard. It startled Buzzy and he lost his balance. He slipped and fell into the pond. He went all the way under. When he came up, he was covered with mud.

Mem laughed and laughed.

"You shouldn't go in the water, Buzzy," Ike said. "There's a snapping turtle in there. It

said. "There's a snapping turtle in there. It could bite off your leg."

Mem laughed harder.

"No, there isn't," Buzzy said. "I was just saying that."

"Yes, there is," Ike said, smiling.

"No, there isn't!" Buzzy said.

"Can you get me a corn dog while you're in there, Buzzy?" Mem asked.

Ike laughed.

"Let's go home," Buzzy said.

They walked across the open field behind the hospital. The sun was hot. It dried Buzzy's mud.

"You look like a salamander," Mem said to him.

Ike laughed. He was having a fun day.

They passed the old weeping willow tree in the middle of the field. Its branches drooped to the ground all the way around.

"Can we go inside?" Mem asked.

"No," Buzzy said. The mud on his nose cracked. "I want to go home."

"Oh, come on," Ike said. "It's hot out."

"No," Buzzy said.

"I won't say you look like a salamander anymore," Mem said.

Buzzy sighed. "Oh, all right," he said. The mud on his chin cracked. "But just for a minute."

They poked through the drooping branches. It was cooler inside.

"Ring inside the willow," Mem sang, "a pocketful of—" She stopped running. "What rhymes with *willow* besides *pillow*?"

Ike thought for a minute. He went through the alphabet in his head, but he couldn't think of another rhyme for *willow*.

"How about *armadillo*?" Buzzy said.

"Good!" Mem said, then ran again, singing, "Ring inside the willow, a pocketful of armadillos. Ashes, ashes, we all fall *down*." And she fell down.

"I still say this would be a great place for a tree house," Buzzy said to Ike.

"What if we brought Mem's playhouse out here?" Ike asked.

"It's too big and heavy," Buzzy said. "We couldn't lift it up into the tree."

"Let's just put it on the ground then," Ike said. "It can be a fort or something."

Buzzy thought for a minute, then he said, "Okay."

"I better ask Mem first," Ike said.

"Ask Mem?" Buzzy said. "Why? It's our stuff!"

"Yes, but it's her playhouse," Ike said.

Buzzy rolled his eyes.

"Mem," Ike said, "is it okay if we bring your playhouse out here under the weeping willow tree?"

Mem sat up. "Sure," she said. "I can make coffee cake for the armadillos!"

Just then the wind began to blow very hard. The tree shook. The drooping branches waved and swooshed.

Ike did not feel a drop.